This book belongs to

© World Rights
Sandviks Bokforlag, Norway
© This edition: **BABY'S FIRST BOOK CLUB**
Illustrated by Marie-Anne Didierjean
Text: Eli A. Cantillon
Cover design: Lene Eintveit
Adapted by Teresa Quirk

ISBN 1-881445-21-6
Printed in Belgium

WILL THE *Elves* COME TONIGHT?

Baby's First Book Club

*T*homas lived with his parents and his grandfather on a farm. He was seven years old and in the second grade. Thomas' best friend was a pony named Sam. Many other animals also lived on the farm: Four cows, two pigs, seven chickens, and a rooster.

One Christmas something very special happened on the farm. It all began on a beautiful, snowy day . . .

It was cold and windy outside, but it was warm and cozy inside the farmhouse.

"Come and sit by the fire," said Thomas' mother when he came home.

"Tell me a story, Grandpa," said Thomas as he climbed up on his grandfather's knee. Grandpa began telling him about the little elves in the forest nearby.

"The elves are curious little creatures," his grandfather began. "The smallest thing can make them angry. If someone forgets to leave a bowl of porridge for them on Christmas Eve, they will play all kinds of tricks on him. They may hide his shoes or spill his orange juice all over the breakfast table."

Thomas laughed. He thought the elves sounded like fun.

"But the elves can be helpful, too," Grandpa continued. "They can talk to the animals, and even know how to heal them when the animals are sick. The elves hide from people, but if you look closely you may see their footprints in the snow."

The next morning, Thomas got up very early. He went to the
stable to take Sam for a ride in the forest. Suddenly, Thomas
noticed some tiny footprints in the snow. He jumped down from
the pony to take a closer look. They looked like the footprints of
tiny children, but Thomas knew that small children would not be
allowed to walk in the forest alone.

"These must be the footprints of an elf!" he thought excitedly.

Thomas and Sam rode home so that Thomas could
get ready for school. Today was the last day before the
Christmas vacation and Thomas was excited because his teacher
had promised to bring Christmas cookies for the class.
Thomas had two friends in his class: Maria
and Andy. They liked to play together,
and Maria and Andy often visited
Thomas on his family's farm.

Thomas ran into the classroom and told Maria and Andy about the tiny footprints he had seen in the forest.

"I'm sure it was an elf," Thomas said. "Grandpa told me there were elves in the forest."

"That's silly," Andy laughed. "There is no such thing as an elf!"

Andy kept teasing Thomas for the rest of the day, but as they were about to go home Maria whispered in Thomas' ear, "Maybe you're right."

Thomas felt very sad. The last day before vacation
had not been as much fun as he had hoped. He went
to the stable to see his pony.

"You are my very best friend," he told Sam. "You
never tease me, and you are always kind." He put his
arms around Sam's neck and gave him a big hug. He
liked to hug Sam with his cheek against Sam's soft,
warm mane.

The next morning, Thomas went to the stable to visit Sam. As he opened the stable door, he saw Sam lying on the floor. When Thomas bent down at his side, Sam could hardly hold his head up.

"Oh Sam, you are sick!" Thomas shouted in dismay, and he ran off to find his parents and Grandpa. They all ran back to the stable with Thomas.

"We have to call the vet," Grandpa said worriedly. Thomas' mother hurried inside to the phone, and came back to tell them that the vet would come out to the farm that afternoon.

Thomas stayed with Sam all morning, nervously waiting for the vet. Then he remembered what Grandpa had told him about the elves being able to heal sick animals.

Thomas decided to go into the forest to find an elf who could help Sam. He called Maria on the phone, and she agreed to help. Maria came right over, pulling her little brother on a sled.

They searched and searched, but could not find a single elf footprint.

"Maybe we should write to them," Maria suggested.

Thomas thought for a moment, and then said, "Let's put up some posters on the trees in the forest."

Maria agreed and they went home to make the posters.

The posters said:

Dear Elves,
Sam is sick. Please make
him well again.
He lives in the stable
on our farm.
Please hurry!
Sincerely,
Thomas

Thomas, Maria, and Maria's
brother tied all the posters to
trees, and then Thomas went
back to the stable. The vet had
come to see Sam, and was just
leaving.

Dear Elves,
Sam is sick. Please make
him well again. He lives
in the stable on our
farm.

Please
hurry!

Sincerely,
Thomas

"What did he say, Grandpa?" Thomas asked.

"He didn't know what was wrong with Sam," Grandpa answered, "but he said he would come back tomorrow to check on him again. I hope Sam doesn't get any sicker before then."

Thomas sat with Sam for hours, reading him stories and singing him songs. Finally, it was time for Thomas to go to bed. He was so tired that he couldn't keep his eyes open any longer. As he walked across the yard from the stable toward the farmhouse, he thought he heard the stable door being opened. He stopped to listen, but everything was quiet.

"It must have been the wind," he thought, and went off to bed.

Early the next morning, Grandpa woke Thomas gently.

"Get dressed and come to the stable with me," Grandpa said.

Thomas jumped out of bed and got dressed quickly. He eagerly ran to the stable, and there was Sam, all well again, looking as if he were smiling at him. Thomas was so happy that he hugged both Sam and Grandpa.

"The elves must have been here," Grandpa said, nodding toward a small stool. On the stool Thomas saw one of the posters that he and Maria had tied to the trees in the forest!

The next morning, Maria came over to visit and she was very happy to see that Sam was well again. Andy came to visit, too. His eyes grew bigger and bigger in surprise as Thomas and Maria told him what had happened.

"You were right, Thomas! Elves do exist!" he shouted.

On Christmas Eve, Thomas brought a large bowl of porridge for the elves out to the stable. He wanted to thank them for helping Sam. Thomas, Maria, and Andy were going to try to stay awake all night to see if any elves came to eat the porridge. But when the elves did come, the children were fast asleep.

To this day no one has seen a real elf. But you can be sure that they do live in the forest. One day some lucky person will spot one. Will it be you?